THE PEOPLE THAT TIME FORGOT

Edgar Rice Burroughs

CAMPFIRE™

KALYANI NAVYUG MEDIA PVT LTD

New Delhi

Sitting around the Campfire, telling the story, were:

Wordsmith	:	Steven Philip Jones
Illustrator	:	KL Jones
Illustrations Editor	:	Jayshree Das
Colourist	:	Vikash Gurung
Colour Consultant	:	RC Prakash
Letterer	:	Bhavnath Chaudhary
Editors	:	Mark Jones
		Andrew Dodd
Research Editor	:	Pushpanjali Borooah

Cover Artists:

Illustrator	:	KL Jones
Colourist	:	RC Prakash
Designer	:	Manishi Gupta

Published by Kalyani Navyug Media Pvt Ltd
101 C, Shiv House, Hari Nagar Ashram
New Delhi 110014
India
www.campfire.co.in

ISBN: 978-81-906963-8-8

Printed in India.

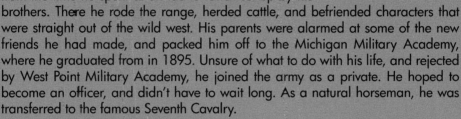

About the Author

Edgar Rice Burroughs was born in Chicago in 1875. He took inspiration for many of his stories from the classical mythology and literature he studied in his youth, and from the time he spent at an Idaho ranch set up by his brothers. There he rode the range, herded cattle, and befriended characters that were straight out of the wild west. His parents were alarmed at some of the new friends he had made, and packed him off to the Michigan Military Academy, where he graduated from in 1895. Unsure of what to do with his life, and rejected by West Point Military Academy, he joined the army as a private. He hoped to become an officer, and didn't have to wait long. As a natural horseman, he was transferred to the famous Seventh Cavalry.

After being discharged from the army due to a medical problem, he returned to civilian life. In 1900 he married his childhood sweetheart, Emma Centennia Hulbert. Following this, he tried his hand at various odd jobs, including being a railway policeman, and a door-to-door salesman. By 1911, he was penniless, with a wife and two children to support. Things were not looking particularly good.

However, his life then took a turn for the better. The story goes that, while proofreading an advertisement for pencil sharpeners in a pulp magazine, inspiration struck. Looking through various magazines, with their tall tales of adventure, he was motivated to write a fantasy story himself. *A Princess of Mars* appeared as a novel in 1912, and his career as a professional writer took off. Another phenomenally successful novel was *Tarzan of the Apes,* published in 1914. The character Tarzan went on to become a legend in his own right.

In 1934, Edgar Rice Burroughs divorced his wife, Emma, and married Florence Dearholt the following year. In 1940, with the war raging in Europe, the couple moved to Hawaii, but this marriage also ended in divorce. Burroughs was too old to be called to active service in World War II. Instead, at the age of 66, he became the oldest war correspondent to serve in the Pacific. He died on 19th March 1950, having written well over 50 novels.

I managed to find Bowen's family business and hand over the manuscript to them. Soon after, Bowen's father unexpectedly died. His assistant, Tom Billings, subsequently organised an attempt to rescue Bowen from Caspak.

There were forty people in the search party. This included the master and crew of the ship known as the *Toreador*.

Tom Billings took full command of the expedition. Raised as a cowboy, Billings had been Bowen's classmate in college, before becoming an assistant to his father.

Billings was determined to find his friend, so we assembled a hydro-aeroplane that he could use to search the island.

We checked the weapons and ammunition thoroughly to ensure that nothing had been omitted.

Soon after Billings flew over the cliff, we heard the sound of his machine gun firing. Then... silence.

We have not seen him since.

It came through the undergrowth and made no attempt to hide itself.

She was the most wonderful being that I had ever seen.

What the...?

I noticed a single armlet between her right shoulder and elbow, and a number of them covering her left forearm. Later I learnt that these were used as shields against knife attacks.

A panther?

It can't be! It's too huge!

RAAARRR

Almost instantly, the biggest cat I had ever seen appeared from the jungle.

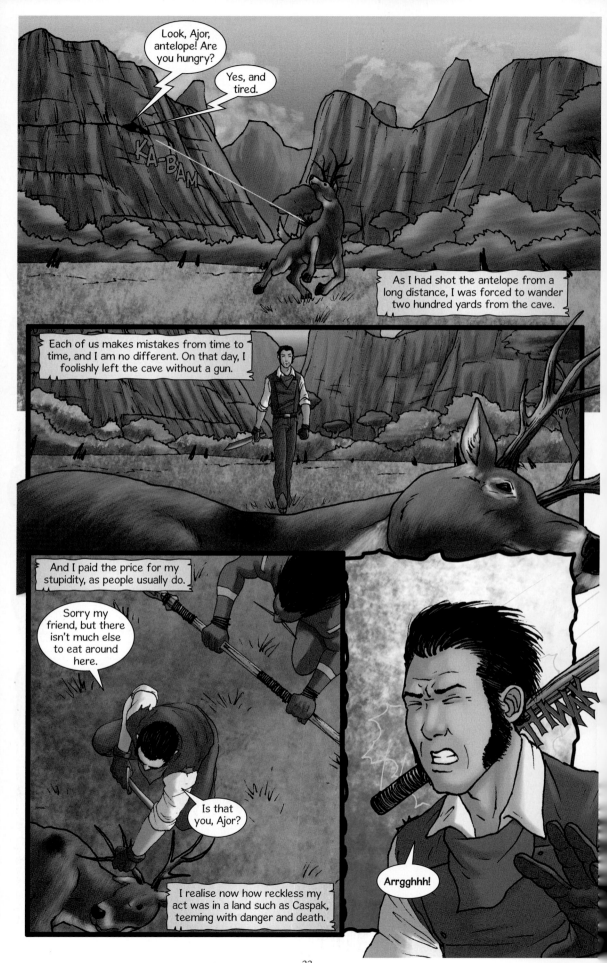

Look, Ajor, antelope! Are you hungry?

Yes, and tired.

KA-BAM

As I had shot the antelope from a long distance, I was forced to wander two hundred yards from the cave.

Each of us makes mistakes from time to time, and I am no different. On that day, I foolishly left the cave without a gun.

And I paid the price for my stupidity, as people usually do.

Sorry my friend, but there isn't much else to eat around here.

Is that you, Ajor?

I realise now how reckless my act was in a land such as Caspak, teeming with danger and death.

Arrgghhh!

28

I couldn't tell if we'd been imprisoned inside the cliff for a day or a week. We were becoming tired and hungry, and the hours were dragging. We had slept at least twice, waking up each time in order to stumble on, getting weaker and weaker.

At times, the corridors climbed upwards constantly. It was heartbreaking work for people as exhausted as we were.

If we were going to die, I would rather it occurred in daylight, instead of the horrid blackness of that terrible cave.

I suddenly awoke out of a troubled sleep, during which I had dreamt that I was falling.

Turn off that light, will you?

A spotlight had formed where Ajor and I were lying. It appeared to be...

This might stop him!

KA-BAM

For a moment, the women were as terrified by the sound of the rifle as they had been by the menace of the cave-lion.

SPLASH

Aiieeeee!

BANG BANG

SPLASH

But when they saw that the loud noise had destroyed their enemy, they cautiously crept back to examine its dead body.

'My father, Jor, is high chief of the galus, but a warrior called Du-seen wants his throne and many newer galus support him.'

'Du-seen also wants me to be his she.'

A cos-ata-lo knows her young will be born as I was, so we are wanted by galu men.

But I don't want any of them... especially Du-seen.

'Not long ago, a spy for my father saw Du-seen speaking with a wieroo.'

'The wieroos offered to help Du-seen take Jor's throne if he gave them all the cos-ata-lo.'

Du-seen would have hidden me from the wieroo if I was his she...

...but I fled to the south to get away from him. I hope my father can stop Du-seen's plot.

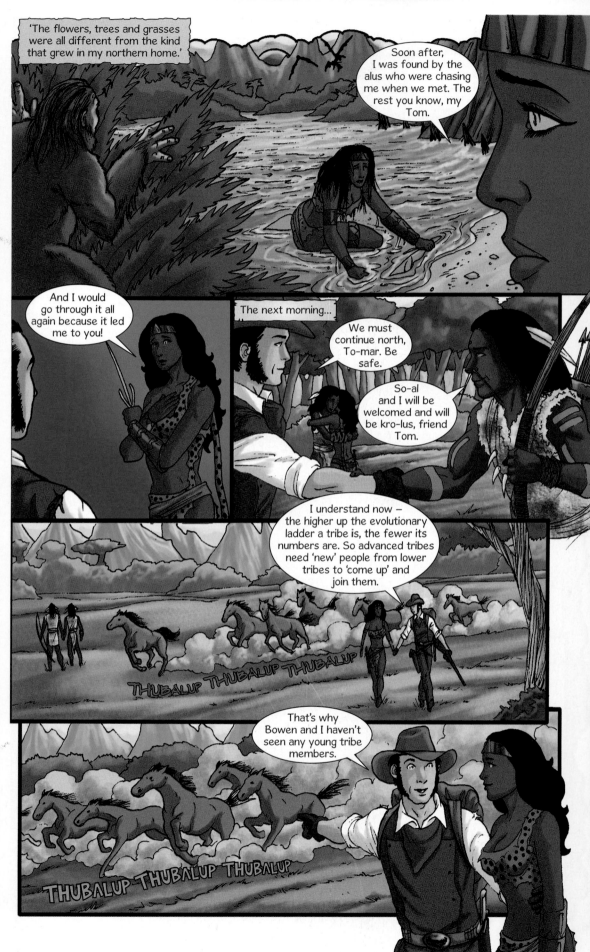

What I still don't understand is what creates life at the beginning.

Are we almost out of these woods?

Ajor and I had gone about a mile or two when, ahead of us, I saw something which caused me to hide.

Band-lus! With a kro-lu prisoner!

He was the first fully developed kro-lu I had seen. He was a fine-looking savage; tall and straight with a regal carriage.

Will they kill him?

Yes. After the dance of death.

No! I cannot allow it.

I shuddered, as I had escaped the same fate. It seemed cruel that someone who had passed safely up through all the frightful stages of human evolution within Caspak, should die just before he reached his goal.

44

...but I think not!

Al-tan and his warriors turned towards me with expressions of immense satisfaction upon their faces.

Think again.

BANG!

I saw that a reply was necessary. So, in one movement, I drew my gun, aimed at the still quivering arrow and pulled the trigger.

This must be my day for good shooting! An arrow makes a mighty small target.

Following my eyes to the tree, the kro-lu tribesmen saw that their chief's arrow was gone. In its place was a large round hole, which marked the path of my bullet.

You see! I spoke the truth!

It was immediately noticeable that my act had an effect on Al-tan, but I'm not sure whether it helped my cause with him. Previously he might have considered me to be harmless and interesting but, by the change in his expression, he now seemed to view me in a new, unfavourable light.

Inside the kro-lu village a friendly crowd of curious warriors and women greeted us.

Chal-az was popular, and the crowd listened to him describe his rescue. Then they thrust necklaces of lion- and tiger-teeth, bits of dried meat, finely tanned hides, and beautifully decorated earthen pots upon Ajor and me.

Al-tan asked me to join him in his council hut, where I met Ajor's enemy.

Allow me to introduce--

My name is Du-seen. What exactly are you?

My name is Tom Billings. What I am is of no concern to you. You don't have a very good reputation, Du-seen.

As I waited for Du-seen's response, I felt something sniffing at my heels, and all of a sudden...

Hey!

As I turned to thrust it aside before it sunk its fangs into me, I saw a huge Airedale leaping frantically. The grinning jaws, the half-closed eyes, and the floppy ears told me this was not a savage enemy, but a joyous friend.

Nobs!

I don't believe it!

I was so surprised to see Nobs, that I checked the name plate on his collar. Sure enough it was him!

Many kro-lus were eager to help Al-tan in his support of Du-seen, but just as many were against the renegade galu's plot.

Al-tan helping Du-seen seemed ironic after he had called my world savage!

Two days into our search, Nobs and I reached the cliffs dividing the kro-lu and galu countries. We followed them for miles, but found no way to get across.

61

64

For the next two weeks, we rested with the galus of Jor. During that time, Chal-az heard his call and came up.

Chal-az later told me that Al-tan and his warriors had been killed when they attempted to re-enter kro-lu territory.

I also learnt that Bowen had married Lys La Rue, and she was now Mrs Tyler.

I guess things had turned out for the best. Ajor and I went out for many rides on Ace. I was never happier.

ABOUT US

It is night-time in the forest. The sky is black, studded with countless stars. A campfire is crackling, and the storytelling has begun. Stories about love and wisdom, conflict and power, dreams and identity, courage and adventure, survival against all odds, and hope against all hope – they have all come to the fore in a stream of words, gestures, song and dance. The warm, cheerful radiance of the campfire has awoken the storyteller in all those present. Even the trees and the earth and the animals of the forest seem to have fallen silent, captivated, bewitched.

Inspired by this enduring relationship between a campfire and the stories it evokes, we began publishing under the Campfire imprint in 2008, with the vision of creating graphic novels of the finest quality to entertain and educate our readers. Our writers, editors, artists and colourists share a deep passion for good stories and the art of storytelling, so our books are well researched, beautifully illustrated and wonderfully written to create a most enjoyable reading experience.

Our graphic novels are presently being published in four exciting categories. The *Classics* category showcases popular and timeless literature, which has been faithfully adapted for today's readers. While these adaptations retain the flavour of the era, they encourage our readers to delve into the literary world with the aid of authentic graphics and simplified language. Titles in the *Originals* category feature imaginative new characters and intriguing plots, and will be highly anticipated and appreciated by lovers of fiction. Our *Mythology* titles tap into the vast library of epics, myths, and legends from India and abroad, not just presenting tales from time immemorial, but also addressing their modern-day relevance. And our *Biography* titles explore the life and times of eminent personalities from around the world, in a manner that is both inspirational and personal.

Crafted by a new generation of talented artists and writers, all our graphic novels boast cutting-edge artwork, an engaging narrative, and have universal and lasting appeal.

Whether you are an avid reader or an occasional one, we hope you will gather around our campfire and let us draw you into our fascinating world of storytelling.

THE MONSTERS THAT TIME FORGOT

PTERODACTYL

The pterodactyl, pronounced 'ter-oh-dak-til' and meaning 'wing finger', was not a dinosaur, but a flying reptile. It originated from the pterosaur group that lived more than 140 million years ago, during the Jurassic period. The pterodactyl would have flown in a similar manner to a bat by using its large leathery wings to glide, and would not have been able to travel great distances. The pterodactyl had a very unusual appearance for the times it lived in. Its teeth were small and pointed forwards, lending weight to the theory that it would have dived for fish, which formed the main part of its diet. It is unknown as to whether the pterodactyl built or lived in a nest.

THE PTERODACTYL'S WINGS WERE COVERED BY A THIN BUT TOUGH LEATHERY MEMBRANE. EXTREMELY LIGHTWEIGHT, THEY ALLOWED IT TO FLY WITH POWER.

WHILE MOST PTERODACTYLS HAD VERY SHORT TAILS, SOME WERE TAILLESS.

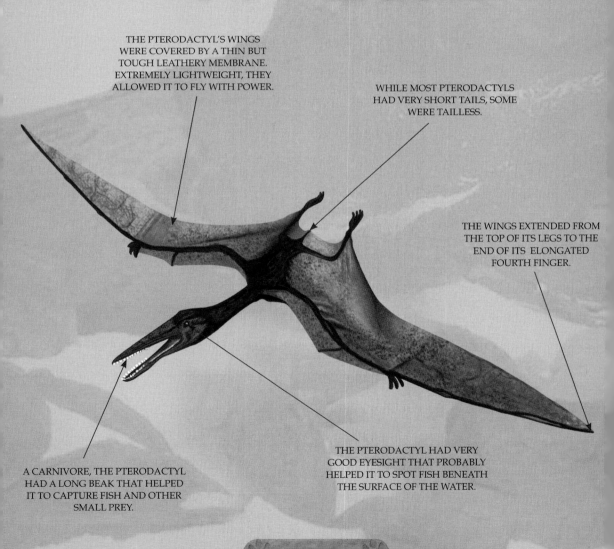

THE WINGS EXTENDED FROM THE TOP OF ITS LEGS TO THE END OF ITS ELONGATED FOURTH FINGER.

A CARNIVORE, THE PTERODACTYL HAD A LONG BEAK THAT HELPED IT TO CAPTURE FISH AND OTHER SMALL PREY.

THE PTERODACTYL HAD VERY GOOD EYESIGHT THAT PROBABLY HELPED IT TO SPOT FISH BENEATH THE SURFACE OF THE WATER.

DID YOU KNOW?

In 1856, thousands of years after pterodactyls became extinct, a newspaper reported that a living one had been seen! Workmen in France claimed to have spotted a large creature with huge wings, black leathery skin, sharp claws and pointed teeth. Those present said that it died and disintegrated into dust. Till this day, its true identity remains a mystery!

SABRE-TOOTHED TIGER

The sabre-toothed tiger was a ferocious looking predator that existed between the Oligocene and the Pleistocene periods (from over thirty million to ten thousand years ago). It was known for its distinctive teeth – two long knife-like canine teeth which had saw-like edges. Different theories exist as to how they were used. Their function may have been to grab and hold on to the prey, or perhaps to inflict a fatal wound. Sabre-toothed tigers were also thought to have lived in packs, and to have had a social structure similar to that of lions. It is believed the extinction of sabre-toothed tigers coincided with that of the mastodons (large elephant-like animals). This suggests that sabre-toothed tigers preyed on these ancient mammals as the main source of their diet.

IT HAD A HEAVIER BUILD THAN MODERN-DAY LIONS AND WAS RATHER BEAR-LIKE IN ITS WALK.

THE SABRE-TOOTHED TIGER'S TEETH COULD EXTEND UP TO EIGHT INCHES IN LENGTH. THEY WOULD PROTRUDE OVER ITS LOWER JAW, EVEN WHEN ITS MOUTH WAS CLOSED.

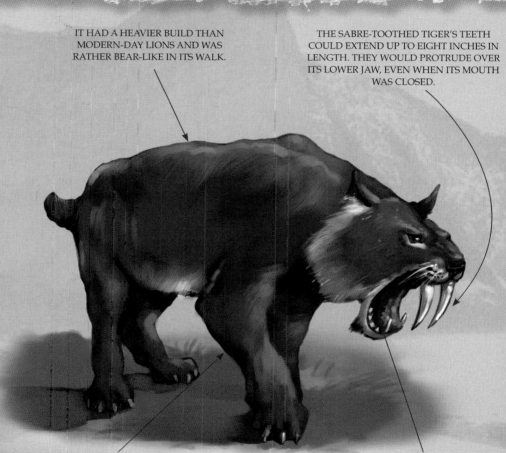

ITS FRONT LEGS WERE VERY STRONG. THOUGH THEY WERE SHORT, THEY WERE POWERFUL AND HELPED IT TO POUNCE ON ITS PREY. THE SABRE-TOOTHED TIGER WAS NOT A VERY FAST RUNNER AND WAS UNABLE TO MOVE AT HIGH SPEEDS OVER LONG DISTANCES. AS A RESULT OF THIS, IT MAY HAVE AMBUSHED ITS PREY INSTEAD.

EVEN THOUGH IT HAD A POWERFUL JAW THAT COULD BE OPENED TO A NINETY DEGREE ANGLE, IT IS SAID THAT IT HAD A RELATIVELY WEAK BITE WITH JUST ONE THIRD THE FORCE OF A MODERN-DAY LION.

DID YOU KNOW?

- Fred and Wilma Flintstone from the American cartoon, The Flintstones, have a pet sabre-toothed cat called Baby Puss.
- In the animated Ice Age films, Diego, one of the main characters is a sabre-toothed tiger who lives with his friends Manfred the Mammoth and Sid the Sloth.